Backyard Bird Watchers

A Bird Watcher's Guide to HUMMINGBIRDS

By Aife Arnim

Gareth Stevens PUBLISHING

Please visit our website, www.garethstevens.com. For a free color catalog of all our high-quality books, call toll free 1-800-542-2595 or fax 1-877-542-2596.

Cataloging-in-Publication Data

Names: Arnim, Aife.
Title: A bird watcher's guide to hummingbirds / Aife Arnim.
Description: New York : Gareth Stevens Publishing, 2018. | Series: Backyard Bird Watchers | Includes index.
Identifiers: ISBN 9781538203156 (pbk.) | ISBN 9781538203170 (library bound) | ISBN 9781538203163 (6 pack)
Subjects: LCSH: Hummingbirds–Juvenile literature.
Classification: LCC QL696.A558 A76 2018 | DDC 598.7/64–dc23

First Edition

Published in 2018 by
Gareth Stevens Publishing
111 East 14th Street, Suite 349
New York, NY 10003

Designer: Laura Bowen
Editor: Therese Shea

Photo credits: Cover, pp. 1 (hummingbird), 12 Ondrej Prosicky/Shutterstock.com; cover, pp. 1–32 (paper texture) javarman/Shutterstock.com; cover, pp. 1–32 (footprints) pio3/Shutterstock.com; pp. 4–29 (note paper) totallyPic.com/Shutterstock.com; pp. 4–29 (photo frame, tape) mtkang/Shutterstock.com; p. 5 gorillaimages/Shutterstock.com; p. 6 Charlesjsharp/Wikimedia Commons; p. 7 Anthony Mercieca/Science Source/Getty Images; p. 8 Ken Thomas/Wikimedia Commons; p. 9 StevenRussellSmithPhotos/Shutterstock.com; p. 11 (top) Annette Shaff/Shutterstock.com; pp. 11 (bottom), 15 Steve Byland/Shutterstock.com; p. 13 KellyNelson/Shutterstock.com; p. 17 Richard Seeley/Shutterstock.com; p. 19 Bonnie Taylor Barry/Shutterstock.com; p. 20 Feng Yu/Shutterstock.com; p. 21 Birdiegal/Shutterstock.com; p. 23 Seaphotoart/Shutterstock.com; p. 25 DanielBehmPhotography.com/Moment/Getty Images; p. 27 Richard Fitzer/Shutterstock.com; p. 29 Sari ONeal/Shutterstock.com.

Printed in the United States of America

CPSIA compliance information: Batch #CS17GS: For further information contact Gareth Stevens, New York, New York at 1-800-542-2595.

CONTENTS

Words in the glossary appear in **bold** type the first time they are used in the text.

MEET ME!

BIRDS I SAW AT THE ZOO

- bald eagles
- falcons
- peacocks
- parrots
- ostriches
- flamingos

Welcome to my bird-watching journal! In school, we keep journals to help us remember facts in science class. I'm hoping this journal will help me remember some cool facts about birds.

Bird-watching is my new hobby. I became really interested in birds after going to the zoo with my class. There were so many amazing birds there! I decided to find ways to get more birds to come to my backyard. That's why I got a hummingbird feeder.

The birds I saw at the zoo don't live in my backyard, but some other cool birds do!

SERIOUSLY SMALL BIRDS

Hummingbirds are totally amazing! First, there are about 320 **species**. That's a lot!

They're not all the same, but most of them are pretty small. There's one species called the giant hummingbird that lives in South America. It's about 8 inches (20 cm) long. That's not too giant! The smallest species is the bee hummingbird. It's about 2 inches (5 cm) long! It only weighs 0.07 ounce (2 g). That's tiny!

RECORD BREAKER

The bee hummingbird is the smallest bird in the world!

Even the biggest hummingbirds aren't so big!

giant hummingbird

THE RUBY-THROATED HUMMINGBIRD

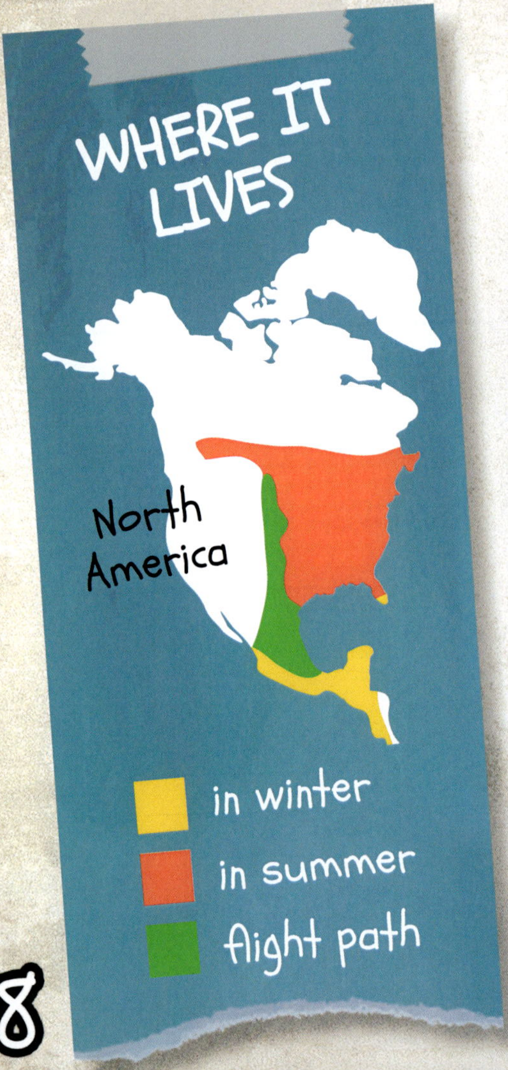

I'd love to see a tiny bee hummingbird, but the closest place it's found is Cuba. That's in the Caribbean Sea. There are about 12 species of hummingbirds in the United States and Canada. The kind that lives near me is called the ruby-throated hummingbird.

In the summer, this species can be found as far north as Nova Scotia, Canada, and as far south as Florida in the United States. It moves farther south in the winter when it gets cold. I made a map to show this!

You can see why it's called the ruby-throated hummingbird. It has feathers on its throat the color of rubies!

FEEDING MY FEATHERED FRIENDS

Hummingbirds get **nectar** from certain kinds of flowers, such as fuchsia (FYOO-shuh). I learned that ruby-throated hummingbirds are drawn to hummingbird feeders. That's why I bought one. I fill it with a sweet nectar that I made.

I hung the feeder near the fuchsia in my backyard. It can take awhile for hummingbirds to find feeders. This one found my feeder pretty fast. I took a picture. Look! You can see how its long bill helps it find nectar deep within a flower.

MY NECTAR RECIPE

4 cups of water

1 cup of cane sugar

Mix it up.

Fill the hummingbird feeder halfway.

Hummingbirds like colors! They seem to really like flower **blossoms** that are the colors red, orange, yellow, and blue.

IT'S A GIRL!

CRAZY!

The sword-billed hummingbird's bill is half the length of its body! What if my nose were that long?

I was so confused yesterday! A hummingbird came to the feeder, but it didn't have a red throat. At first, I thought it was a new species. My mom said I should look up the ruby-throated hummingbird on the Internet. I found out something cool.

Only male ruby-throated hummingbirds have a red throat. Females don't. So the bird I saw was a female ruby-throated hummingbird. Both males and females have greenish feathers on the top of their head and back and have a grayish belly.

Not all hummingbird species have males and females of different colors, but most do.

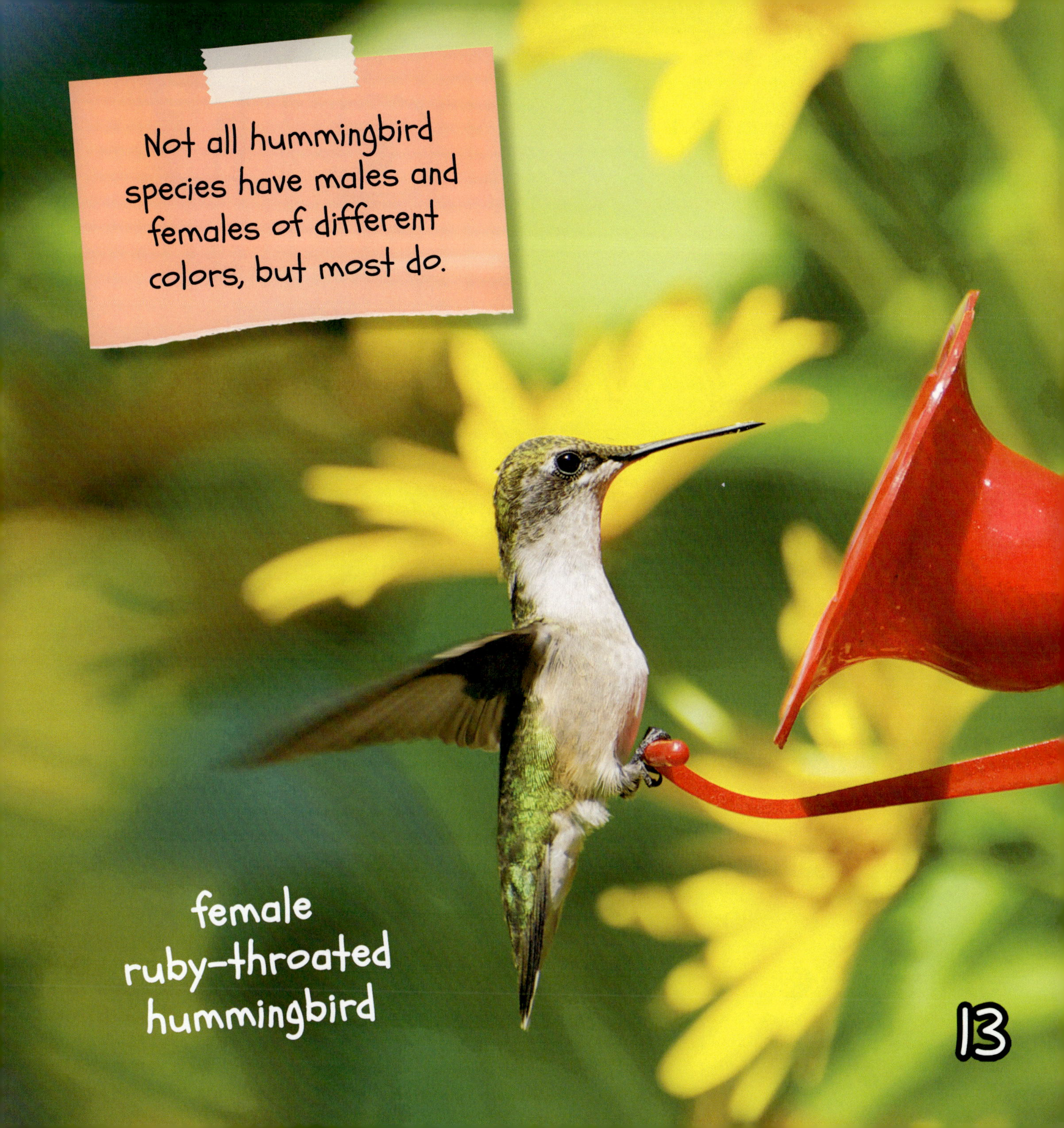

female ruby-throated hummingbird

WINGING IT

FUN FACT!

The larger the hummingbird, the slower the wingbeat rate is.

My photos show that hummingbirds have short wings. That doesn't mean the wings aren't powerful. They let the bird fly forward, backward, straight up and down, and sideways. I love watching a hummingbird hover. That's when you can see how fast it beats its wings.

I couldn't even count a hummingbird's wing flaps—that's how fast they are. I had to do **research** to find out how fast they flap: 70 times per second!

The wings are flapping so fast that they look blurry in this photo Dad took. I could hear the wings "hum"!

TOUGH BIRDS

LISTEN!

A hummingbird's call sounds like this: *chee-dit!*

I was watching the hummingbird feeder from my window when I saw a male hummingbird dive at another male. They weren't playing. One of them lost a few feathers! The other squeaked and then dove again. That squeak meant "GO AWAY!"

I found out that hummingbirds are territorial. That means they don't like other hummingbirds coming into their territory to eat, especially during **mating** season. They let females come in if they're looking for a mate.

I borrowed Grandpa's phone to take this picture of two hummingbirds fighting! Males and females sometimes fight, too.

PICK ME!

A male hummingbird shows off so he'll be picked as a female's mate. He dives in the air again and again, and zips back and forth. He puffs out his red throat feathers. He might beat his wings even faster, too!

There's a male and female in our yard, so I think they're mates—since they're not fighting! Ruby-throated hummingbirds have babies between March and July. Tomorrow I'm going to look for their nest.

Hello, Good-bye!

Hummingbird mates only stay together a few days or weeks.

Bird lovers sometimes call ruby-throated hummingbirds "RTHUs" for short!

I SPY THE NEST

NEST AREA

2 inches (5 cm) across

1 inch (2.5 cm) deep

I found the hummingbird nest today! It was at the end of a branch so it wasn't hard to spot. I was looking up at it, so I couldn't see into it. I could tell the nest was made out of plants.

I didn't want to scare away the bird—I know that's a bad idea. I looked up hummingbird nests on the Internet. The mother hummingbird makes her nest from plants and puts **lichen** or moss on the outside. That sounds comfy!

I saw this photo online and printed it out for my journal. This hummingbird is called an Anna's hummingbird.

SUPERSMALL EGGS

BIRD WORD!

incubate (IHN-kyuh-bayt): to sit on eggs to keep them warm so they'll **hatch**

The hummingbird nest is small, but the eggs are really small! They're just 1/2 inch (1 cm) long. The hummingbird mom lays her eggs when she's done making the nest. She usually lays one to three eggs. Then, she incubates them for about 2 weeks.

The mom gets hungry, though, so I see her zipping back and forth to the feeder and the flowers for a quick meal. She has to make it fast. The eggs won't hatch if they get too cold.

Hummingbirds sometimes use spider webs to keep their nests together! Cool!

CHICKS!

From my house, I can see that the hummingbird eggs have hatched. And I can see two chicks poking their heads up! They're opening and closing their beaks. They're hungry! Since they've just hatched, their eyes are shut, and they don't have many feathers. They can't leave the nest—or they could get eaten by blue jays or cats!

The mother feeds them a couple of times per hour. She hasn't been coming to the feeder, though. She's giving them bugs that she catches and chews up. Eww!

HUMMINGBIRD BUG GRUB!

beetles
flies
bees
mosquitoes
mites
wasps
spiders*

*extra tasty to them!

Here's a photo of a hummingbird nest in my neighbor's yard.

GROWING UP AND MOVING OUT

TRACKING HUMMINGBIRD TIME

number of days to build nest: 6–10

number of days between eggs being laid and hatching: 12–14

number of days hatched chicks stay in nest: 18–22

I saw the hummingbird chicks leave the nest for the first time! They're about 3 weeks old. They flew down with their mom. She took them around to places they could find food. I read that she'll help them for a few days and then make them find a new place to live. She might mate again and lay some more eggs.

Male hummingbirds aren't as mean about sharing their territory after mating season is over. Hopefully, it won't be hard for these birds to find enough food!

It's hard to know if young hummingbirds are male or female. They don't grow their adult feathers until winter.

HAVE A GOOD TRIP!

I haven't seen the male hummingbird for a while. He must have flown south already. In the fall, hummingbirds fly south to Mexico and Central America. Some **migrate** as far as 500 miles (800 km)!

I make sure there's lots of nectar in the feeder so the hummingbirds can eat before they go. They'll need **energy**. They may not stop until they get to their winter home. I hope the hummingbirds come back next year!

FLOWER POWER

Hummingbirds spread **pollen** from one flower to another. That helps plants make seeds so that new plants grow.

Before migrating, hummingbirds store energy for their journey in a layer of fat. A hummingbird may double its weight!

GLOSSARY

blossom: a flower of a seed plant

energy: power used to do work

hatch: to come out of an egg

lichen: a plantlike growing thing found on rocks and walls

mating: coming together to have babies

migrate: to move to warmer or colder places for a season

nectar: a sweet liquid produced by plants

pollen: a fine yellow dust produced by plants

research: to study to find something new

species: a group of animals that are alike and can produce young animals

FOR MORE INFORMATION

Books

Harris, Tim, ed. *Birds*. Redding, CT: Brown Bear Books, 2011.

Hirsch, Rebecca E. *Ruby-Throated Hummingbirds: Tiny Hovering Birds*. Minneapolis, MN: Lerner Publications, 2016.

Otfinoski, Steven. *Hummingbirds*. New York, NY: Cavendish Square, 2015.

Websites

Guide to North American Birds
www.audubon.org/bird-guide
Find out about different species of hummingbirds and other birds.

Ruby-Throated Hummingbird
www.allaboutbirds.org/guide/Ruby-throated_Hummingbird/id
Read more facts about this amazing bird.

Publisher's note to educators and parents: Our editors have carefully reviewed these websites to ensure that they are suitable for students. Many websites change frequently, however, and we cannot guarantee that a site's future contents will continue to meet our high standards of quality and educational value. Be advised that students should be closely supervised whenever they access the Internet.

INDEX